BI
21
BI
Te   **Dyer** is the award-winning author and illustrator
 (br   *Fiends*, *Mrs Muffly's Monster* and *A Monster Day at Work*.
Batty   th book and she has been published in over nine countries.
          ld never hang upside down for very long as a child
          s great at making friends. She lives in Hove, England.

for:

Otto Arthur
Maddie Noah
Jonas Elsa
Jacob Ruben
Jacob Mollie
Nancy Belle
Sean Owen
Eve
Amy
Beth Sam
Edie
Charlie
Jack Hollie
Ollie Poppy
Amalia Theo
Freya
Charlie Josie

A catalogue record for this book is available from the British Library.

ISBN 978-1-84780-159-3

The illustrations in this book are pencil and pastel

Set in Myriad

Printed in Shenzhen, Guangdong, China by C&C Offset in November 2010

1 3 5 7 9 8 6 4 2

First published in Great Britain and the USA in 2011 by Frances Lincoln Children's Books, 4 Torriano Mews, Torriano Avenue, London NW5 2RZ www.franceslincoln.com First paperback published in Great Britain in 2011

BATTY

Sarah Dyer

F

FRANCES LINCOLN
CHILDREN'S BOOKS

Batty isn't the most popular animal at the zoo. All he can do is hang upside down.

"hello"

LONG
EARED
BAT

His efforts to impress the visitors are always unnoticed. He is determined to try to be popular like the other animals.

GIRAFFES

LIONS

The penguins are having fun in their pool.
Batty wants to join them.

He dives in!

"*Blerch*" splutters Batty.

The water is freezing and he realises that bats don't like fish. Being a penguin isn't such fun after all.

Next he comes to the gorillas. They look friendly.

Hmpf thinks Batty.

Perhaps they are a bit too friendly.
He is sure he doesn't have fleas.

Moving on, Batty arrives
at the Lion's Den.
This looks very relaxing.

"*Phew!*" sighs Batty.

It is far too hot and bright in the
sunshine for his tiny eyes.

tweeeeet

Not giving up, Batty lands
in the Tropical Aviary.
All the birds look so beautiful.

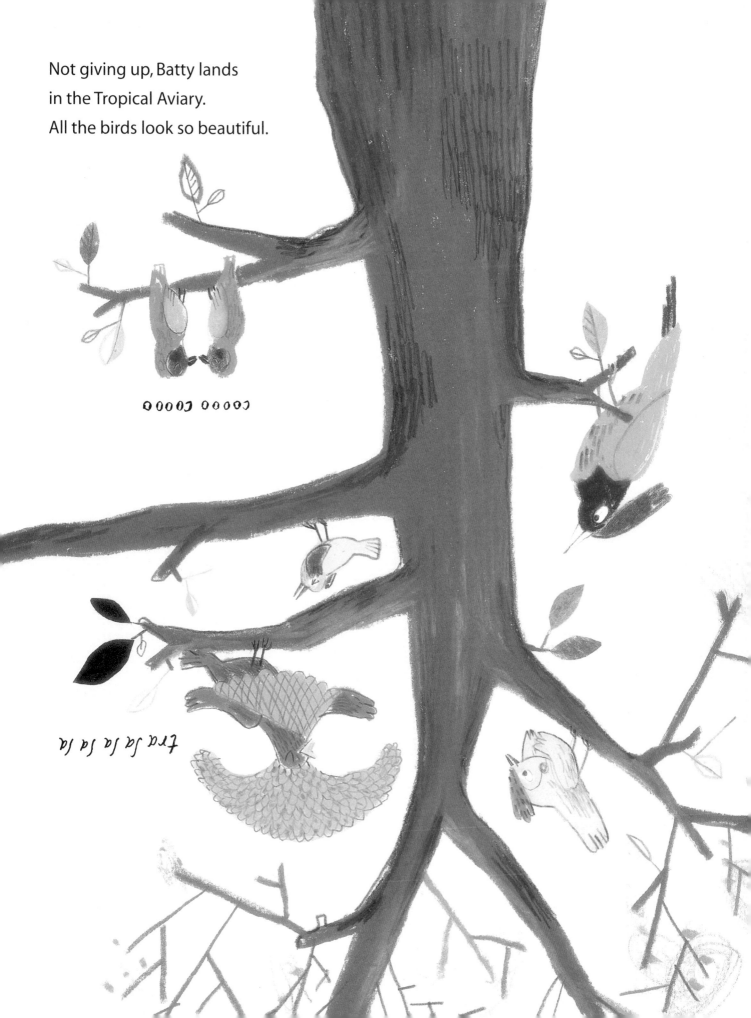

"*Eeek,*"
squeals Batty.

Up close it is far too noisy for his sensitive ears.

Feeling sad and lonely,
Batty flies back to his home.

When he gets there,
all the animals he has met
have come to visit him.
Batty realises that he is also
good at making friends.

MORE TITLES BY SARAH DYER
FROM FRANCES LINCOLN CHILDREN'S BOOKS

MRS MUFFLY'S MONSTER

Mrs Muffly lives by herself in a house on top of a hill. She has always been a bit strange, but lately she has been acting very, very strangely indeed. Could this be because she is keeping a HUGE monster in her house?

"Executed with great flair and warmth." – *Books for Keeps*

"5 stars - Sarah Dyer's humorous and fantastical text is perfect for reading aloud together or for newly independent readers." – www.bettybookmark.co.uk

MONSTER DAY AT WORK

Little monster spends a day at work with his father. First he has to dress and choose which tie to wear. Then he must travel with Dad and all the other commuters. At work he eats the biscuits at the meeting, colours the graphs his father makes on the computer, goes to the canteen for lunch and even stops off for a drink on the way home. Monster thinks his father has it easy at work.

"Full of fun and humour . . . this is playful entertainment with a cast of amiable but oddball creatures." – *Junior*

"Packed full of charm and humour." – www.writeaway.org.uk

Frances Lincoln titles are available from all good bookshops.
You can also buy books and find out more about your favourite titles,
authors and illustrators on our website: www.franceslincoln.com